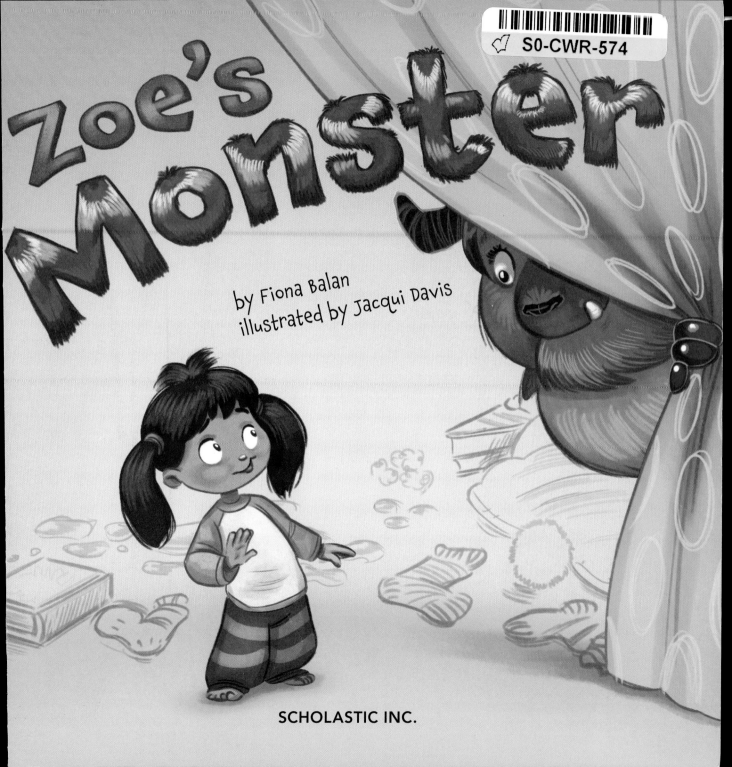

Zoe's Monster

by Fiona Balan
illustrated by Jacqui Davis

SCHOLASTIC INC.

Written by Fiona Balan. Illustrated by Jacqui Davis. Designed by Dorothea Lee.

Copyright © 2018 by Scholastic Inc.
All rights reserved. Published by Scholastic Inc. Printed in the U.S.A.

ISBN-13: 978-1-338-28415-7
ISBN-10: 1-338-28415-0

SCHOLASTIC and associated logos are trademarks and/or registered trademarks of Scholastic Inc.

2 3 4 5 6 7 8 9 10   40   27 26 25 24 23 22 21 20 19

Scholastic Inc., 557 Broadway, New York, NY 10012

One night, on her way to bed,

Zoe began to suspect that **something** was not quite right.

The next night, as she lay down to sleep,

Zoe **knew** that something was not quite right.

On the third night,
that *not-quite-right* thing kept her up very late with its **loud** snoring.

On the fourth night,
that thing made a **GIGANTIC** mess.

By the fifth night,
Zoe knew exactly what was going on.

There was a **Monster** under her bed.

Zoe's Monster was **not** very nice.

In fact, it was rather **rude**.

When she
turned **out** the lights,

the Monster turned them
right back **on.**

And just as she started to fall asleep,

the Monster would get up and have a **dance party**.

That's when Zoe
knew she had to do
something
about it.

She was going to
catch the Monster.

First, she tried to sneeze
the Monster out with dust bunnies.

But instead of **out**...

the Monster sneezed **up**.

Next, she tried to lure it out with a delicious monster treat.

But the Monster was...

too fast.

Then Zoe tried to tease it out with a toy.

But the Monster was...
too strong.

Finally, she tried to suction the Monster out with a vacuum cleaner. But it was...

too smart.

Just as Zoe
decided to give up...

...she heard a voice,
very close to her ear.

"**Ok!**"
the Monster answered.
"*I love playing
with you.*"

And so...

they did.

Goodnight, **Monster**.

Goodnight, **Zoe**.

Try This!

Silly monster books are lots of fun. For even *more* fun, try the tips below!

1) Catch a Monster

Zoe had a great monster-catching plan. Too bad none of her ideas worked! Do you have any other good monster-catching ideas? Be sure to draw a picture of your plan.

2) Monster Play!

At the end of the story, Zoe and her Monster have lots of fun. What are some other fun things they could have done?

Now it's *your* turn! Grab your favorite monster (adult or child!) and have some fun, monster style.

Facing Fears

Monsters and nighttime (the dark) can be scary. Here are some ways to help your little monster face and overcome fears:

- **Listen & understand.** Talk together about your child's fears. Ask questions; discuss his or her thoughts. Share your own childhood fears and how you learned to be brave.

- **Have fun in the dark.** Put on a flashlight show, play games, or "scare" your child's monster silly by crouching at the bed and saying, "BOO!"

- **Use "monster spray."** Fill a spray bottle with water. Let your child know that this powerful spray is guaranteed to keep away lurking monsters.

- **Make friends with your monster,** just like Zoe in the story! After all, what do little monsters really want to do? Play?! Ok!